Contrary
Imaginations

Larry Callen

Contrary Imaginations

≈ GREENWILLOW BOOKS ≈
New York

Library of Congress Cataloging-in-Publication Data
Callen, Larry.
Contrary imaginations / Larry Callen.
p.   cm.
Summary: When their mother can't decide where
to dispose of their father's ashes, three children
take matters into their own hands.
ISBN 0-688-09961-0   [1. Fathers—Fiction.
2. Brothers and sisters—Fiction.]
I. Title.   PZ7.C134Co   1991
[Fic]—dc20
90-33181   CIP   AC

To a bunch of Callens:

Willa, Erin, Alex, Dashiel, Holly,
Emily, Lawrence, Dorothy, David, Ann, and Toni.

To Leticia Rochelle (Rocky) Maya Callen,
because first grandchildren are special.

To Patricia Padgett and Gary Mouton,
whose box in a closet triggered the idea.

Especially to Alex David Callen, the seeker.

Contents

Contrary
Imaginations

≈ **C H A P T E R   1** ≈

Time to Say Good-bye

Two fathers are one father too many.

Alex, Mom, and the twins sat at the kitchen table. It was a family meeting, and they'd had them before. But this one bothered Alex. It was the first time they had ever discussed a subject more serious than rules or homework or where to spend Christmas.

The subject was Big Al, Mom's friend, the first man friend around the house since the divorce a bunch of years ago. Alex clearly remembered the day Dad had hugged him tight and then walked away.

"Mom, how could anybody *not* like Big Al?" asked Lily. She was painting her nails blue. It was a lark, and as soon as the polish dried, she would remove it. Lily knew Mom wouldn't let her out of the house with blue nails. "He's interesting-looking and funny and probably rich." She held up her nails, blew on them, and examined them. "And, Mom, you've got to realize that if God didn't want you to meet Big Al, then you would've never met him."

Lily liked bringing God into conversations. It was her way to add authority to her arguments. Most times Alex thought what Lily said was funny, but Lily was not one to try to be funny when God was making the argument.

"I like him, too, Mom." Joel had been floating a vanilla wafer in his glass of milk. It sank out of sight as he talked. He quickly glanced at the second hand of his watch. His aim, Alex knew, was to break his record for floating time. All of the wafers floated briefly, then soaked in milk and sank. By using a delicate touch to place the wafer on the surface of the milk, Joel delayed the time the wafer actually began absorbing milk. Joel reached for another wafer. Then he looked at Mom.

"Maybe what I like best is he shakes my hand and doesn't frizzle my hair," Joel said.

"I get hugs," said Lily, smugly smiling at Joel.

"I get hugs," said Joel. "Sometimes I get hand-shakes, too."

"I get hugs all the time," said Lily.

"All right," said Mom. "I'll put in an order with Big Al for more hugs for Joel and more handshakes for Lily."

"No, Mom!" the twins shouted.

Mom's eyes shifted to Alex. The flicker of a smile that had been on her face disappeared. Alex was the oldest. The twins had no memory at all of Dad. But Alex remembered. Some things he remembered he would rather forget. There were lots of loud arguments. Most things he remembered were nice. But

Dad was gone. Alex hadn't seen Dad since Dad left. Mom said money came regularly, and Alex and the twins got cards on birthdays and Christmas signed "Love, Dad." More would have been nice.

"How do you feel about Big Al, Alex?"

It was an easy question to answer if the subject was only Big Al, not Big Al's replacing Dad.

"Mom, you know I like him a lot. We play ball, and he took me rabbit hunting a couple of times, and he's fun to talk to."

What Alex didn't say, and the true reason he liked Big Al, was that Big Al made his mother smile. For the first few years after Dad left, Mom seldom smiled. During the past year that she had known Big Al, she was Mom again. Big Al was good for Mom. But Alex wasn't yet sure that was the same as Big Al's being good for him and Lily and Joel. Most of the kids he knew who had substitute fathers didn't get along with them very well.

Alex also wasn't sure what would be proper for him to say at this particular family meeting. Mom was sounding them out. She was doing it casually, but if Big Al weren't important to her, she wouldn't be doing it at all.

So, thought Alex, do we talk about Dad right now, or don't we? And as he asked the question, he answered it. Better to talk about Big Al. There would be other times to talk about Dad.

"Is Big Al coming over?" Alex asked.

Mom smiled. "Yes, he's coming over. And we're going to the movies, all of us. Who wants to see *The Mummy Returns*?"

Lily's blue-fingernailed hand shot up in the air. Joel dropped a cookie in the milk, and the angle caused it to sink almost immediately. Up went his hand.

Alex smiled a yes at Mom. It was a thoughtful thing for Mom and Big Al to do. Mom knew the twins loved horror films. Alex didn't care for them at all, but Mom had no way of knowing that since he had never told anyone. Alex knew Mom and Big Al would surely choose another movie if this weren't a family outing. It was nice of them, and Alex intended to do his best to help make it nicer.

Maybe a new family was taking form. For the millionth time since his real dad left Alex wanted to talk to him. Now it was too late to ask him to come back home. Maybe this time Alex only wanted to say good-bye.

≈ C H A P T E R   2 ≈

The Tester
of the Rules

Alex hadn't expected it to be a good book. Most times the books recommended by the kids at school were duds. This one wasn't exactly recommended. It was sitting on top of a scarred classroom desk. His eyes flicked over the worn cover of the book.

Contrary Imaginations, the title said. The book was a tattered softcover, much read. He flipped through the pages, then settled on one. And then one more. Something was being said here that he wanted to understand. He replaced the book on the desk.

The title wasn't in the school library. But he found it two days later in the public library. Some people, said a character in the first chapter, are born to test the rules. If the rules are solid, they hold. If the rules are weak, they fall, and new rules are formed. Different people have different ideas about what the rules should be. The book gave examples of famous people who had tested the rules in religion, politics, science, and elsewhere in various phases of learning. But *Contrary Imaginations* was a book of fiction about a man who tested the rules in another area.

As Alex continued to read, the idea began to grow in his head that kids were normally asked only to listen and obey. The character in this book, though not a kid, followed a different path.

The first chapter ended. Alex found a more comfortable position in his chair, moved the desk lamp a bit to provide favorable light, and settled in for an enjoyable afternoon of reading.

The phone rang shrilly. It was an interruption. It wasn't a call for him. It seldom was, unless Tisha called. But he waited a moment before beginning to read. He didn't want the second chapter to pull him into the book and then have to stop reading to pass on a homework assignment to some dimwit who hadn't paid attention in class.

He heard hard black plastic clack against hard black plastic as his mother hung up the phone. And then her shaking voice sounded from the kitchen.

"Alex, I need you." It was a call for help rather than a command. Reluctantly he marked his place in the book and closed it.

His mother moved back and forth between the cupboard and a picnic hamper which sat on the kitchen table. She was packing food. For a moment he watched her. She was medium height. He was now as tall as she was, and next year he would be taller. She was wearing a pale blue dress. It was a Sunday dress, even though this was a Saturday afternoon. She liked nice clothes. Alex had watched her from a distance before. The only mars to her beauty were the fine lines beneath her eyes, increasing gradually as do the annual rings of a tree. He had first noticed the lines soon after Dad left.

"We're going to visit Granny Victoria," she said.

"Ahhh, Mom!" He wanted to get back to his book. And he and Tisha had talked about going to the movies. "I've got a date with Tisha tonight."

"Well, you call her and say I'm kidnapping you, and I'm sure she'll understand. I'm packing a few things so we don't have to buy food on the road. Round up Lily and Joel. Have them do some packing. Lily should bring her books, and Joel his games. You can read or write your stories. I want to leave soon so we can be there well before dark. We'll be back tomorrow afternoon."

When he realized he could continue reading the book during the ride, his thinking changed. A trip to Granny Victoria's would be fun. They would be at the Gulf of Mexico. There might be time for a walk on the sandy beach, perhaps a chilly swim.

Lily and Joel were even more excited about the trip.

"But I won't go unless Mom promises we can have boiled crabs on the way," Lily said. She pushed brown curls from her forehead. One strand of hair lingered, and she blew it away from her eyes.

"Mom is packing canned tuna and crackers so we won't have to spend money," Alex told her. Boiled crabs would have been nice. Maybe they could catch their own crabs when they got to the Gulf.

"Then I'm not going," Lily said.

"Okay," said Alex. "But pack, anyway. Both of you." He smiled at Joel, and Joel winked back at him. Alex left the room. His mother would need more help in the kitchen.

Mom wasn't impressed with Lily's threat.

They packed the hamper of food and the water

jug in the backseat. The box with the change of clothing went into the trunk.

Mom opened the back door of the car, then stared at Lily. Lily stared back. The staring match lasted fifteen seconds. Lily took a step toward the car door.

"All right, Mother, I'll go." She entered the car and plopped down on the backseat. Mom closed the door with a snap of her wrist. "But I'm not coming back," said Lily.

≈ C H A P T E R 3 ≈

What's Happening at Grandma's?

The first forty miles, after they crossed the Huey P. Long Bridge over the Mississippi River, was flatland. Cows and green sugarcane. Alex sat in the front seat with Mom. He settled into his book.

"Beep!" went Joel's computer game. "Beep! Beep!"

The main character in *Contrary Imaginations* was a man named Constantin. He had a theory that dreams are real and life is not. He spent a great deal of time talking to this old bearded Chinese person.

"There are things man was meant to learn, and there are things man was meant not to learn," said the old bearded Chinese person. "What man was meant not to learn, man will never know."

Constantin's argument was that with practice, man can learn to control his dreams but man cannot learn to control his life. Therefore, life is subservient to dreams.

"Beep!" went Joel's computer game.

Alex cringed, but he didn't say anything. He tried to block out the beep. He watched the fields and the cows flash by.

"Beep!" went Joel's computer game.

"Mom!" said Lily.

"Lily, did you see the horses?"

"Where?"

"Look out the back window and to the left. Under the trees."

"Mom, I don't see anything at all."

"Well, dear, next time I'll try to tell you sooner."

There were few automobiles on the road. There was only the sound of puffing wind at the windows and the steady hum of the motor.

"Mom, I'm trying to read, and Joel's beeping all over the place," said Alex.

Joel's eyes rose from his computer game. "I'm close to a record score," he said. "This talk is distracting me."

"Mom, I can't read with all this noise."

Alex had lost his train of thought with every beep. Constantin was about to embark on a new adventure into the world of dreams. Alex was ready to follow.

"Mom, I want you to pay attention to what I'm going to say," Lily said.

Mom nodded. So did Joel and Alex. Sometimes Lily seemed desperately serious about what she said, and always when she was, it was funny, although she seldom saw the humor.

"Mom, you remember what Dad used to say?"

The motor noises were the only noises to be heard.

"Actually, I don't remember hearing him say it. You told us he said it. He said there is a piece of God in each and every one of us. You remember that, Mom?"

Mom nodded slowly. Her attention was on navigating around a mile-long truck, but the slowness of her nod indicated her attention was partly divided.

"What you told us, Mom, was if there is a piece of God in each of us, then each of us must act Godlike, right?"

Joel was staring at her out of the corner of his eye. He had stopped fiddling with the computer game. Alex knew the minute Joel was able to figure out the way Lily's thoughts were headed, the beeping would begin again.

Mom nodded, and Lily continued. "Well, Mom, it's clear that's wrong. If there was a piece of God in Joel, he wouldn't be distracting me from my book. Reading is fundamental, Mom. That's what they say on television."

Alex had hoped for more.

For a while there was quiet as they drove past miles of green cane fields.

Alex went back to his book. Constantin had decided contact with earth is what befuddles the mind and makes humans believe the dreamer dreams the dream instead of the dream's dreaming the dreamer. So Constantin must achieve a special kind of flight to detach himself from the surface of the earth.

"Mom," said Lily, "look at Joel. There can't be any of God in Joel. He's picking his nose."

Alex smiled. They were passing a Burger King. He was reminded he was hungry, but canned tuna and crackers and warm water would have to do the job. He kept silent.

"Horses on the left," said Mom.

Lily hadn't a word to say as she watched the field of grazing horses. In time flat grassland gave way to watery trails, and soon there was swamp on the left and swamp on the right. White cattle egrets circled and lit. Joel's eyes were fixed on his computer game. Alex desperately wanted to learn more of Constantin's exploration of flight from the surface of the earth and into the world of dreams. Mom's full attention seemed focused on driving the car down a cement ribbon of highway which radiated afternoon heat.

Alex knew this wasn't so. Her attention was elsewhere. For the first time since the trip began, he wondered why they had set out for Granny's so quickly. They had made the very same journey only last month. A few hours ago Mom received the phone call, and almost minutes later they were on their way. Was everything all right at Granny's?

He didn't plan to ask such a question in front of Lily and Joel. But if they stopped for gas, he was surely going to ask.

"Mom," said Lily, "if God did pick his nose, how large do you think the booger would be?"

≈ **C H A P T E R 4** ≈

Lily's Mission
in Life

Constantin's early efforts at flight were primitive. He later realized he had merely transferred the experience of floating in water in an inner tube to floating in air in an inner tube. Air took him where air wished. He wanted more control.

Constantin returned to the old bearded Chinese

person, who raised his eyes to the sky and said, "The first step on a journey to the stars begins on earth. And the last step, also."

The thought brought peace for a moment, and then Constantin's mind plunged onward. And Alex's mind did, also. Chinese philosophy, Alex thought, is much like Chinese food. One hour later you are hungry for more.

"More horses," said Mom.

Alex had no interest in seeing horses, but his head involuntarily flicked up.

"Mom, those are cows," said Lily.

"Mom, could we have quiet, please?" asked Joel. "This time I'm really going to break my record. This is important, Mom."

They moved past marshlands, crossing small silver bridges every mile or so. Then they left the four-lane highway for a two-lane road, and Alex knew his reading time was at an end. For the remainder of the trip they would be following Bayou Lafourche toward the Gulf of Mexico. Small settlements dotted the bank every few miles. Shrimp boats ten times longer than the car, with names like *Mama Mia* and

Love Boat and *Alphonse Cheramie,* were docked on its banks. Occasionally a single boat chugged toward or away from the Gulf. Constantin must wait awhile. These boats held contrary imaginations of their own and caused other interesting dreams to be dreamed.

"Mom," Lily said shrilly, "did I abandon all my rights as a woman when I unwillingly entered this car?"

Alex shifted in his seat and twisted around. "Lily, be quiet."

"Mom," Lily continued, "all the good things to see are on the right side of the car, and Joel is just sitting there going beep, and he won't change seats with me."

Alex looked at Mom, grinning, shaking his head. Mothers suffer in strange ways.

Mom had been quiet for a long while now. Nothing on her face showed she thought the situation funny. Her mind was part on the driving and part someplace else. There was a crispness to her tone when she answered. "Joel, put your toy away or change seats with Lily."

"Mom, this isn't a toy. It's a computer. My

teacher said the world's future depends upon computers and on people like me understanding their
possibilities."

"Beep."

"Besides, this time I'm really going to set a new
record."

"Joel, don't make me stop the car to settle this."
It was a warning, and he should have paid attention; but he didn't.

"Beep."

The car began to slow down.

"Okay, okay, she can have my seat!"

But the car continued to slow down. There was a
gasoline station ahead. Mom pulled in and stopped
at the nonleaded pump. She switched off the en-
gine.

"Everybody out," she ordered.

Alex went to the pump and began filling the tank.
Joel looked at Mom, waiting for a tongue-lashing,
but none came.

"Bathroom time," she said.

The tank was filled, and the gasoline paid for, but
Joel and Lily had not returned.

"Mom," said Alex, "why are we going to Granny's?"

She hadn't expected the question. Her eyes moved slowly to him. Alex saw pain in her face. It was a pain brought on by something other than the bickering of the kids.

"It's a visit," she said.

"We're in an almighty hurry to get there for just a visit," said Alex.

"A visit," she said. "Granny needs company. We'll do more talking when we get there."

"Mom . . ."

"We'll talk later, Alex. Here come the kids. . . . Who wants tuna and crackers?" Mom asked.

Nobody did.

Lily claimed the window seat nearest the bayou, and Joel didn't say a word. He let his computer talk for him.

"Beep, beep."

Alex wondered what there was to talk about that Mom didn't want to talk about now. Maybe Granny was sick. But if she was, why was it a secret? He wondered what was going on this very moment inside Mom's head.

"Ugh!" said Lily.

The car had rushed past a dead animal on the side of the road.

"It looked like a dog," said Lily.

"Could have been a possum," said Joel.

"It was too big for a possum," said Lily.

"Possums come pretty big, Lily," said Alex. "Bigger than cats."

"It was a dog," said Lily.

There wasn't enough interest in the subject to keep the bickering going. There was silence in the car. Even the beeping stopped, as Joel focused his attention on the boats chugging down the bayou.

"Mom," said Lily, breaking the silence.

"Yes?"

"Does God have a dog?"

Mom's face softened, and she smiled for the first time since they had set out on their journey.

"Oh, Lily, such a question."

"Well, what's the answer?"

"I'm sure God has a dog if God wants a dog."

"Well, do dogs go to heaven?"

"Maybe Granny will know," said Mom.

"Mom, that poor dog is lying there beside the road, totally dead, and nobody is praying over him, and he will never, never get a proper burial." She looked out the back window of the car. "Mom, I think I know what I want to do with the rest of my life."

Only Joel had the boldness to ask.

"I'm going to become a missionary and convert dogs to become Catholics, that's what."

A hush.

"Mom?"

"What?"

"How do I do that?"

Small Step,
Giant Step

There was a long quiet. Alex heard a shuffling in the backseat. Then Lily cleared her throat.

"Mom, if the world were Catholic, and if dogs truly liked meat, what would dogs do on Friday?"

Another long quiet. The car hummed background music as all waited for an answer to Lily's question.

Alex realized the truth was that there wasn't an answer in the bunch. Lily's mind was playing with reality. She was focusing on possibilities even Constantin might want to consider days from now. Joel's mind was part on his game and part on Lily. Joel liked having a twin like Lily who explored all the possibilities and didn't have a glimmer about any of the answers. Mom's mind was on something known only to her. Alex's mind searched futilely to discover whatever Mom's mind was on.

They whizzed past miles of cane fields, shrimp boats, twists in the bayou. Things were normal outside the car, and yet things didn't seem normal inside the car. Lily's concerns should have been entertaining enough to be distracting to Alex, but they weren't.

What was happening at Granny's? It was important to know.

The car rolled smoothly, if noisily, toward the Gulf of Mexico. Soon, Alex hoped—more than hoped, knew—he would learn more.

Mom, why aren't you telling me what I want to know right now?

Mom, why do I feel that I don't even know the proper questions to ask?

And then, in the distance, he saw Granny's house. It was large, almost castlelike, lifted from the gritty sand of the Gulf's beaches on foot-thick dark brown wooden pilings. Alex loved climbing the splintery wooden steps, sand popping out of his shoes with each hesitant step.

What was Granny going to tell them? Did Mom already know? They had moved too quickly for this to be only a pleasure trip.

He took a single step out of the car. He braced for whatever. His mind made quirky associations. He suddenly remembered the astronaut stepping from the lunar landing module onto the surface of the moon and saying something about a small step being a giant step. Did it fit what was about to happen to him now?

The Gloom
in the Den

G ranny Victoria's house was filled with cheer-
ful light. The windows were large and
screened and open most of the year. The furniture
inside was old and easily transportable during hur-
ricane season. The front porch faced the sandy road,
and the back porch faced the pounding waves of the

Gulf. Alex had once heard his mother tell a friend that if you didn't like plenty of sun, you didn't like Granny's house.

Granny Victoria herself could not have stood up to a brisk wind. She was a short woman, thin, strong, and brown-skinned like many people who lived under the sun on Louisiana's Gulf Coast. But what she lacked in size she made up for in spirit and a sharp voice when things didn't go her way. Alex had often thought that he respected Granny because she was his father's mother, and he loved her because she was Granny.

Lily and Joel gave Granny Victoria a hug and ran for the shore, with Mom yelling "don'ts" at them. Alex wasn't even a tiny bit tempted to go. Now he would learn the reason for the trip.

There was a pot of steaming coffee on the stove, and soon the three of them sat at the table. Granny stirred the hot brew.

"Only half a cup for you, and plenty of cream," Granny Victoria said to Alex. She tolerated his drinking coffee at her table as long as she was the one who decided how much cream he put into his coffee.

Alex took his first sip. Hot. Sweet. He was about to take another sip when he realized his grandmother's eyes were on him. He set the cup down on the table.

"Alex," said Granny Victoria, speaking softly, "your mother already knows. There's no easy way to say this, boy." She hesitated a moment. Then the words came out in a cadence. It was as if she had rehearsed what she would say next.

"Your father died a week ago, Alex. I learned about it only this morning."

Now he knew. He had thought about his father often over the years. His knowledge of why his father had left was slim. He knew that his mother hadn't wanted his father to leave.

Granny was still talking.

". . . and what's left of him is in the den."

Granny Victoria's words drained blood from his veins and poured in hot lead. His body was suddenly so heavy he couldn't move. Not one single lead-filled finger.

"You all right, Alex?" his mother asked.

He couldn't even nod.

"I was telling your mother, boy, that your father

died in a hospital in Pensacola. He must've been there awhile because they got two wishes out of him."

His desire to go into the den and see his father was overpowering. Was his father lying in a coffin, hands folded across his chest? Was he on the sofa, a pillow tucked under his head? Alex pushed his chair back. The sound of wood scraping against wood shivered his spine. He stepped toward the door.

"We ought to do more talking first, Alex," said Granny Victoria.

But his mind was no longer in control of his legs. Some inner being lifted one leaded foot and then the other from the floor.

He stood in the doorway of the den and scanned the room. There was no coffin. There was no body on the sofa. There was nothing out of the ordinary in the room. Sofa. Chairs. Card table surrounded by folding chairs. A small brown cardboard box sat on one corner of the card table.

"There's more to be talked about, Alex," said Granny.

He glared back at her.

"Where is he?"

"Come sit, boy."

His strong legs moved him back to the kitchen table.

"Your dad told the hospital he wanted to be cremated, and he wanted the ashes sent back here."

Right!

His mind went back to the gloom of the den. The battered cardboard box on the corner of the card table contained the ashes of his father.

He wanted to go back into the den again, but he didn't dare. His father was no longer real. No longer touchable. It was a thought too big to think. His mind thrust it out. Nonsense cluttered his head.

And then his mind took hold again, and he realized his mother was sitting across the table from him, crying soft tears. His wasn't the only loss. He stood up, walked slowly around the table, and cloaked his arms around her. Then his own tears flowed.

≈ **C H A P T E R   7** ≈

I Don't Know
What to Do

Lily's reaction was philosophical.

"I can't imagine that God wanted each of us to be only ashes in a box, Mom." She paused. "Mom, you have to tell us more about Dad."

Joel was having a problem with the fact that his father, who used to be somewhere else, was now here and somewhere else at the same time.

"Are you sure it's him?" he asked.

Alex, a million years ago, had tried to accept the fact that he no longer had a father. Maybe he no longer needed someone around the house who could toss him a ball. Maybe he no longer needed someone who could camp with him in the woods. Maybe he no longer needed someone who could listen to him when there was something he wanted to say but he didn't know how to say it. Too many "maybes" to be true.

"What do we do now, Mom?" Alex asked.

They ate supper. When you live on the Gulf, you eat lots of fish. Potatoes go well with fish. But Alex had no appetite. He glanced at the others. When you mix potatoes and fish and grief, you get only grief. The meal was over almost as soon as it began.

"The dishes can wait," said Granny Victoria. They gathered on the wooden back porch, let the cool winds of the Gulf soak in, and watched the sun fade to a pink sky, then to darkness.

"Your father loved it here," Mom said. "We used to sit and do just what we are doing now. We would watch the shrimp trawlers coming in from the Gulf, and we would watch the helicopters carrying people back and forth from the offshore oil rigs out there too far away to see. The helicopters looked like ugly wingless birds during the daytime, and they looked like floating, sparkling stars at night. Your father always wanted to ride in a helicopter. I wonder if he ever did."

"What do we do now, Mom?" asked Alex again.

She looked at him for only a moment. Then her eyes moved to Granny.

"Victoria, what do we do now?" she asked.

"Getting kind of cool out here. Want to go in?" asked Granny.

"No."

Granny sat there, staring into the darkness. A sleeve moved up to dab her tears. When she talked, there was a crack in her voice, but soon the strong voice of the old Granny returned.

"Mary Dorothy, you listen. I've loved only three men in my whole life. I dearly loved my father. He gave me values, and he gave me strength. I loved my husband. He changed me from a child into a woman, and he helped change your husband from a child into a man. And I loved my one and only son.

For sure, he taught me how to give of myself. It's the nature of children to teach that. He made his share of mistakes, but there was never a more lovely man. Mary Dorothy, you know that's true."

Mom sat there nodding that she felt the same way.

"Well, Mary Dorothy," said Granny, "the ashes were sent to my address, because he was my son, but it was your name that was on the box. He wanted you to have a say-so. I think he just wanted me to be there when you decided."

The darkness was there. The light coming from the kitchen windows silhouetted each of them, but faces were gone. Alex listened closely to the words. What should they do with the brown cardboard box? That's what they were talking about. What *can* you do with a box full of the ashes of your father?

What would Constantin do with such a box? Maybe that question was easier to answer than it first appeared. Surely Constantin would dream a dream in which the box disappeared and the ashes became the man, and the man sat on this very porch in this very darkness at this very moment.

Surely the man in the box would strum a guitar and sing a silver song, and the music would sail out over the beach and roll with the waves toward open water, where his voice would join the dreams of all the things which swim.

Alex had pulled the guitar out of an old memory.

"Remember when Dad used to sing 'Down in the Valley'?" Alex said.

Lily's sweet, high voice started in on the song almost immediately—"the valley so low. Hang your head over, hear the wind blow. . . ."—but no other voice joined hers.

She stopped singing. "Come on, sing!" she said, and began again, but still no one joined her.

"All right, then I'll sing by myself." She started over once again and sang the song to its very end.

When she finished, there was soft applause from Mom. "Thank you, Lily. You have honey in your voice."

Alex sensed the song had changed the mood. Mom's voice was steady. Briefly at least her mind had been on Lily's song.

"Victoria," Mom said to Granny, "we have at

least two choices. I can take him back home with me, and we can bury him in the family plot next to Grandpa. I know both of them would like that. Or we can let him spend his days right here on the Coast. This was a special place for him."

"There's no cemetery for miles, child," said Granny, "and we aren't going to plant him in my backyard. The neighbors would talk if I started my own private graveyard."

"We could scatter his ashes on the waters of the Gulf," Mom said.

Decisions
by Candlelight

Candles were appropriate. Each of them lit a candle. The air was cool but still. The only sound was the roar of the surf, and it seemed a subdued roar to Alex. Crashing chords of organ music were right for a funeral. This was a quiet funeral.

At the rear of the house, and above the line of

high tide, a wooden walkway stretched three steps up into the air and then straight out a hundred feet across the waters of the Gulf. At the end was another wooden porch. The walk and the porch were bordered by a cypress rail.

Guitar music. Where did it come from?

Many a sunny day Alex sat on that porch, high above the water, listening to the water slap at the creosoted poles which supported the porch. In the distance he watched dolphins play. Many a lucky day also he threw a fishing line and caught a red snapper or two.

And then from deep in memory again came the sounds of the guitar. His father sat on the rail, daintily plucking a tune, but Alex's mind had pointed not on the tune but on the fact that if his father leaned a bit too far backward in support of his tune, his father would plummet into the realm of the dolphins. And his father and his father's guitar, filled with salty water, would make no more sound.

"This doesn't feel right," said Mom. "Let's go back to the beach."

They retraced their steps. The wooden boards

made noises in the night. It was like stepping on the keys of an organ, but the organ knew why they retreated and merely groaned. They stepped off the hard wooden boards and onto the soft, crunchy sand.

They sat in a circle. Each punched a finger in the damp sand and then planted a candle deep into the hole. They made a ring of light, with a cardboard box in the middle, and each sniffed the tartness of salt and candle smoke in the air.

"What's all this sitting for?" said Granny Victoria. "If we are going to do something, let's do it."

"This cardboard box is hard to open. I should have brought a knife," Mom said. She tried a fingernail, but the seal wouldn't budge.

"Mom," said Alex, "is Dad sending us a message?"

"What we need, Mary Dorothy, is a shell with a sharp edge," said Granny Victoria.

"Mom," said Joel, "isn't it time for me to go to bed?"

"Somebody find a shell with a sharp edge," said Mom.

Nobody moved.

Then Alex touched the damp sand and felt something hard. He cupped it in his fingers. He probed the grittiness of the sand. Sharp edges. It was half of an oyster shell.

"Mom," said Alex, "I've got a shell."

"Give it to me." The candlelight danced on her face. It wasn't a happy face. Alex felt the night breeze. He listened to the sound of the waves. There are only five people in the whole wide world, he thought. Me and Mom and Granny and Lily and Joel. And we five are trying to decide what to do about Dad. Would we want the same people deciding what to do about us?

Probably we would.

And if we could have another person deciding, Dad would be here also.

"Mom, please don't open the box," Alex said.

"Mom, God's telling us what to do and we ought to do it, whatever it is," said Lily. "Alex, give Mom the shell."

But Mom didn't move to take it.

"Mom," said Joel, "I'm truly sleepy."

In the millions of years that there had been a world, surely there had also been times when a small group of people sat around a fire and made important decisions. Alex glanced from candle to candle. All five candles wouldn't be much help if a saber-toothed tiger approached. But their decision didn't concern something physically threatening to the five of them. It was a more foreboding threat. Their decision would affect not when they died but how they lived.

Granny Victoria took the shell from Alex and handed it to Mom, who made a rip into the seam of the box. What was inside? An urn of ashes? A plastic bag of ashes and bones which hadn't burned to a crisp? Alex thought he heard the sound of something snapping when the box had been tilted.

Alex listened to the gentle slosh of the water against the pilings. In only moments his father would be gone. There would be handfuls of him scattered out over the water. He would flit on top of the waves. The fish would frolic. The thought occurred to Alex as it occurred to Lily, and Lily was quicker to express her displeasure.

"Gross!" said Lily. "It will be like feeding flakes to the fish in an aquarium. God wouldn't want this!"

Alex cringed with each of Mom's soft tears. He shed soft tears of his own. He had worked hard toward accepting that he no longer had a father. But he knew, also, that he wanted what he understood of his father to be close enough to talk to anytime Alex needed to talk. And the more Alex thought about again having a father, the more he realized there were so many wonderful new things to talk about.

"Mom, let's not do this," said Alex. "Don't open the box. We should go home. And we should take Dad home with us. That's where he wants to be."

≈ C H A P T E R   9 ≈

The Eraser
of the Pain

Constantin abandoned efforts at flight when he accidentally discovered the TV remote control. Surely that was the appropriate way to control both dreams and reality. If the present isn't satisfactory, you can Reverse. If what you are doing isn't what you should be doing, you can Pause. If what's happening isn't as exciting as what could be happening, you can Fast Forward. And you can Stop. If you Stop, you get the opportunity to Start all over. Constantin played with the Stop button the most. He controlled time.

And then he realized he was always avoiding the present, not affecting what had been or what could be, and Constantin went back to day one.

But Alex didn't. Alex dearly began to wish for his own remote-control device which could erase the pain which started when a real dad became a non-dad.

"Victoria, it's time for us to go home, and I want you to come back with us," Mom said. "There's going to be a burial one way or the other, and I know you will want to be there when it happens."

Granny's suitcase went in the trunk, and the twins, Granny, and the cardboard box went in the backseat. Alex could never remember seeing Granny sitting in the front seat of a car.

There were differences of opinion before the automobile even moved out of the driveway.

"Mom, you can't expect me to sit back here with this box between me and Granny, can you?" said Lily. "Why can't we just put it in the trunk?"

"Mom," said Joel, "please don't put the box between *me* and Granny."

Mom screeched the car to a stop and twisted around in the seat.

"Mary Dorothy," said Granny. "I'm not exactly sure I want to sit next to this box, either. I rocked him in my lap when he was a child, but things just aren't the same."

There was something close to anger on Mom's face.

"Mom," said Alex, "this box belongs in the front seat."

Mom was always quick to speak her mind. This time it was as though she weren't sure what her mind was. And it was causing her pain.

Nobody had ever made rules about what was

right and wrong in such a situation. But Alex now knew what was right for him.

"Front seat," he said. "For sure it's where he would have been if he were . . ." And the words trailed off, and a guarded stillness returned.

The Story Granny Told

At first the ride home was a quiet one except for Granny Victoria's directions to Mom on how to drive the car.

"Mary Dorothy, watch out for that truck!"

The day lengthened, and soon the twins were asleep in the backseat. Mom had her eyes on the road, her ears on Granny's backseat driving, and her mind a third place. They had filled the gas tank shortly after leaving Granny's, so there would be no need to stop.

"Mary Dorothy, we seem to be going mighty fast around all these dangerous curves."

The light was fading, and Alex was in no mood to read *Contrary Imaginations*, but still Constantin was inside his head. It was curious. Alex knew he was there, but Constantin did nothing to call attention to himself.

"Mary Dorothy, is it time to turn on the head-lights?"

The twins began to stir.

"Mary Dorothy, aren't you following that car mighty close?" asked Granny.

"Mom, could we stop for a hamburger?" asked Joel. "It's been hours and hours since I had any-thing to eat, and I'm dreadfully hungry."

"Well, Joel, we'll get you home before you die of dreadful hunger, I promise you that." Mom gave him a reassuring nod and a smile.

"Watch the darned road," said Granny.

While Alex's mind had been on Constantin, the cardboard box all but disappeared from the seat between him and Mom. Then the sound from the backseat brought him back to reality. He suddenly realized one elbow rested lightly on the cardboard box. The box was real. That was when he was certain what was happening wasn't a dream, so Constantin would play no role in the outcome.

Yet his next thought was that he might need Constantin's help. What then?

Lily was strangely quiet. Not normal. Soon that changed.

"Granny Victoria," Lily said, "I want you to tell me a story."

"Yes!" said Joel, and promptly forgot about hamburgers.

Granny Victoria smiled at Lily. "I'll do it," she said, "but it will have to be a short one because I have to help your mother with her driving."

Alex glanced at Mom, but she merely smiled, and then Lily was talking again. "I want you to tell us a story about when Dad was courting Mom."

"Lily!" Mom shouted.

"It's all right, Mary Dorothy. You just pay attention to what you are doing. I have plenty of stories to tell. Some of them you haven't even heard." Granny Victoria cleared her throat. "Mary Dorothy, I'm going to tell the one about the bicycle trip from New Orleans to Yellowstone Park. You won't mind hearing that one again, I'm sure."

Alex had heard the story a bunch of times, and the trip kept getting longer each time Granny told it.

Granny took Mom's silence as an indication she wouldn't mind hearing the story again. "Well, I'll start off, and if I forget something, Mary Dorothy, you pitch right in. But as we ride, *do* keep your eyes on the road. I don't want to end this day in a cardboard box of my own."

The story's beginning was always the same.

"You children know your dad and mom had been teenage sweethearts. Then your mom's family moved to Shreveport. Your mom and dad were brokenhearted. One day your dad told me and your grandpa—your dad was maybe seventeen and kind of snippety—that he was old enough to go on a summer vacation all by himself. He had saved his money from after-school work at the fertilizer plant, and he was going to visit Yellowstone National Park. And since he didn't have too much money, he planned on traveling on a bicycle. And he planned on stopping at Shreveport along the way."

"I never heard the part about Yellowstone Park before," said Lily.

"Well, I can't help that," said Granny Victoria. "Mary Dorothy, watch out for that truck!"

"Granny, is it really true about the bicycle?" asked Joel. Shreveport was about four hundred miles away, and Yellowstone was about fifteen hundred miles away.

"Sure, it was a bicycle. Balloon tires, regular old-fashioned bicycle. But he never made it all the way to Yellowstone. You know what happened next?"

Everybody knew what happened next, but they wanted to hear it from her. Granny looked first to Joel, then to Lily, then to Alex, then to Mom, then to the road. The road was clear, so she continued.

"He got as far as Shreveport all right. Took him almost a week. Then he bought a second bicycle for about ten dollars, proposed marriage to your mom, and the two of them came home on bicycles about a month later as man and wife."

"What happened to Yellowstone?" asked Joel.

"It didn't seem very important at the time," said Mom.

Alex liked to hear this story about his father. It made his father seem real. Both he and his father had bicycles. Both he and his father had girlfriends. Alex suddenly remembered he had forgotten to call Tisha and cancel their date.

Flickering
Between Channels

"Wake up, children," Mom said in a weary voice as they pulled into the driveway. The sun had set. There was a stirring in the back-seat.

Alex opened the door on his side, then reached across and took the keys from the ignition. He stepped out of the car, lifting the cardboard box from the seat.

"I'll go and unlock the front door," he said.

Once inside, he flicked on the lights, then stood in the center of the room and looked around. What to do with the box? It was the first decision he'd had to make since leaving Granny's.

There was a small table normally used as a desk for homework in one corner of the front room. He pushed a few books to one side and set the box on the table. Something was wrong. It didn't fit. He moved the box slightly, making it equidistant from all sides of the table, and then it fitted. He backed off and faced the others as they entered the room.

Mom's eyes flitted past Alex and to the table. "Good. Now, let's all go to the kitchen for a peanut butter sandwich and milk, and then to bed."

But Alex couldn't sleep. He switched on the light and began to read his book. Constantin was still flicking between dream channels. The minute he found fault with one channel, he changed to another. And then another. Tens, hundreds, soon to be thousands of realities whirled by. Then Constantin put down the remote-control device and, looking directly from the printed page into Alex's eyes, said, "Dealing with more than one reality at a time makes me dizzy."

Alex rubbed his eyes. When a character in a book begins talking to you, it's best to get some sleep. He put the book on the bedside table, and he put his head on the soft pillow. When sleep didn't come promptly, he remembered the game Constantin had been playing. He flicked realities in his mind. He did it with a rhythm, as if he were counting sheep. Soon he slept.

Time for
the Show

In the morning it was breakfast as usual. The bacon and eggs and butter and grits smelled and tasted good, maybe even better since Granny did the cooking. The chatter of the twins was about the same. The cardboard box in the front room governed the thoughts in Alex's mind, but it was Mom who was going to have to decide what to do, and Alex was resigned to wait.

The twins soon abandoned the kitchen for the backyard. Alex cleaned off the table. Granny Victoria sat at one end, fidgeting uncomfortably because she had nothing to do.

"Mary Dorothy, you know you can bury him in the family grave with Grandpa," said Granny Victoria.

"Thank you, Victoria. I'm just totally lost right now."

She went to the phone in the front room. When she came back, she didn't pick up a dish. She slumped on a chair at the table.

"I called three different funeral parlors. Nobody wants to deal with a box of ashes when I don't even have a death certificate. So I called the cemetery, and they want several hundred dollars merely to shovel a hole in the grave."

Slowly she straightened her shoulders. Her head moved, and she stared directly at Alex.

"I'm tempted to dig the hole in the hard dirt myself," she said.

The back door was suddenly flung open, and Lily and Joel rushed in, followed by two of their friends. A third friend, a tall, thin girl, stood rigidly on the porch, not entering the kitchen.

Lily and Joel and their two friends walked hurriedly through the kitchen. Mom's voice stopped them.

"Where do you think you're going?"

They came to a halt. Lily stared at Mom. Joel stared at the floor.

"Into the front room," said Lily.

"It would be better if you and your friends played in the yard," said Mom.

"We'll go out in a minute. I promise," said Lily, moving toward the door.

"Lily!" The warning was softly stated but clear. "What's going on?"

Lily wasn't too happy with the question. Mom's eyes dared her not to answer.

"They want to see the box. I promised them one quick look."

"For a quarter each," said the boy.

Mom walked quickly to the kitchen screen door and flung it wide open.

"Out!" she said to the boy and the girl. They were quick in complying, but on the porch, with the screen door again shut, the boy's nerve returned.

"What about our quarters?" he asked.

Lily looked to Mom, then hurried to the door and handed out the quarters. Two of the children ran. The third continued to stare through the screen into the kitchen. Mom noticed and went to the door.

"Well?" she asked.

The thin girl's voice shook as she spoke. "Is there really a dead person in a box in the living room?"

"Yes, there is," Mom said.

"Oh, Lord," said the girl, then suddenly spun and fled.

Lily and Joel spent the rest of the day in their rooms. Periodically the quiet would be interrupted with a plea to go outside.

"Mom," said Lily, "we didn't tell a lie, we didn't cheat, we didn't break a single commandment, and we're being punished all day long. What kind of children do you expect to have if you punish them for telling the truth?"

Later she tried again.

"Mom, we did it because we love Dad so much. We wanted our close friends to know how much we love him. If they saw him, then they'd know we really must love him if we keep him in a cardboard box in the front room."

And again.

"Mom, we were going to give the money to the church on Sunday."

And one last time.

"Mom, it was Joel's idea."

A Final Resting Place

The twins were still in their rooms. Mom and Granny were washing vegetables for a supper salad when the phone rang. Mom went to answer, then came back with a jumbo smile on her face.

"It was Big Al. He's coming over for a visit. I'll put on a pot of coffee."

The first time Alex realized Mom thought anything special about Big Al was when he showed up, invited and with a present, at the twins' last birthday party. He was a tall, balding, stocky man who occasionally shot basketball hoops with Alex and shared basketball stories.

The twins ripped the fancy wrapping paper off the large box, and inside was a typewriter.

"It's a kind of family present," said Big Al. "Your mom told me you twins were learning to type on computers at school. I know Alex likes to write his stories. And your mom can use it for letter writing, or whatever."

Big Al got hugs from some, handshakes from others, and he got at least one kiss.

When the doorbell rang, Mom rushed to the door and came back into the kitchen towing Big Al by the hand.

"Coffee's ready," Granny said. She eyed Big Al. She had seen him before. They shook hands limply and politely.

And then, before Big Al had a chance to take a single sip of coffee, Mom tightly squeezed his hand

and began telling him about the trip to the Gulf and the box in the front room and her calls to the funeral parlors. There were tears streaming from her eyes and a sob in her voice. Soon she placed his strong hand on the table, leaned over, and rested her head on Big Al's hand.

Alex watched. Big Al was responding to his mother's feelings. He spoke softly to her. The sobbing stopped. Mom sat up straight, dabbed at her eyes with the end of the tablecloth, and struggled to smile. When the smile came, Big Al stood up slowly.

"Excuse me for a moment," he said. He walked out of the kitchen toward the front room. The footsteps stopped. Alex could imagine him standing in the front room, staring at the box of ashes. What was he thinking? The footsteps returned. He sat down, nodding his head.

Alex found it comforting that Big Al was staring at him rather than at Mom. Big Al reached out and gripped Alex's shoulder. Then Big Al looked at Mom.

"Mary Dorothy, I can't advise you what to do.

But you ought to decide quickly. That box is going to cause anguish and it's going to cause disturbance within this family until it finds a final resting place."

The coffee cups sat on the table, coffee getting cold.

"Let's take a walk," he said.

They returned an hour later. Big Al said good-bye at the door. Mom came into the kitchen, where Alex was trying his best to get interested in Constantin's adventures, but his mind wouldn't let him.

Mom sat at the table, head shaking side to side.

"Big Al's a dear man," she said. "He wants what's best for me. We talked and talked and talked. He said he's heard of people who had ashes scattered from a boat on the Mississippi River or even in Lake Pontchartrain. He said there are 'scatter' gardens in some of the local cemeteries. He said he even knows of a man who had the ashes of his wife buried in his backyard. He said he thought burying your dad in the family plot was the best idea. He said there's only one wrong thing I can do. And that's not to do something quickly. That box can't stay in the front room."

Her eyes focused on her hands as she talked. Then she looked at Alex.

"Everything he says is true. But I still don't know what to do."

"Mom, what's causing the problem?"

She folded her fingers in front of her. She moved a single finger to her temple, as if there were a tiny pain. One hand then covered her mouth for only a second. The other dropped to her lap. It was as if she had no control over what her hands were doing.

"I just know your father had something in mind when he sent the ashes to me. And I don't know what it is."

≈ C H A P T E R 1 4 ≈

The Rainbow Possibilities

Mom finally put her fingers back to work on the leafy green salad that was to be supper. Alex watched briefly, then returned to his book. Before he had read to the end of the chapter, for the first time he fully realized the significance of the title: *Contrary Imaginations*. It came out in another conversation between Constantin and the old bearded Chinese person. Constantin had drawn a square in the middle of a white piece of paper. He then blackened the square with the pen.

"Black on white," he said.

The old bearded Chinese person smiled.

"My eyes tell me one thing, but my imagination tells me something contrary," he said.

Constantin was puzzled, and so was Alex. Then Alex realized that one reality could have been black on white, as Constantin said it was. Another reality could have been white on black, if only a white sheet with a square hole in the middle lay on top of a black sheet.

Alex went into the front room and stared at the cardboard box. Maybe he only thought he knew what was inside.

"If only I knew what to do," said Mom.

Alex closed the book.

"We should bury him in the family plot," Alex said. "Granny Victoria says it's the right thing to do. I think so, too. And you would think the same if you were thinking regular. What else is there to do? What could he possibly want you to do that you haven't thought of doing? Mom, he wasn't trying to torment you. He just wanted to be close."

Mom sliced a fat red tomato and put the thick wedges into a dish on the table.

"You're probably right, Alex. That's what we should do."

When the salad was ready, Mom called Granny. Lily and Joel arrived as if by magic.

"Joel, put glasses all around, and Lily, pour the root beer."

Lily talked as she poured. "Mom, I think we made a mistake by not burying Dad at the beach. He loved it there, Mom."

"Lily," said Alex, "it was you who said we would be feeding the fish."

"Not in the muddy Gulf water, Alex."

"There won't be any holes dug in my backyard," Granny Victoria said. "I was serious about that."

"On the beach! On the beach!" said Lily. "You can sit on the beach and see white sand and blue waves and the golden sun rise and set. You can see practically everything between Louisiana and China."

They scooped green salad into dishes, thinking of the rainbow possibilities of the Gulf. Mom poked at her salad, then put her fork back down on the table.

"Maybe you're right, Lily. He did love it there." She looked across the table at Alex. "He did, Alex. He did."

When the dishes were cleaned and put away, Granny and Lily and Joel moved to the television. Alex stayed at the kitchen table with his book. Mom sat across from him with a deck of cards, endlessly playing solitaire. Alex wondered if the game afforded her time to think or if it afforded her time not to think.

Constantin had come to the conclusion that if black and white existed on two planes, or on the same plane, or didn't exist at all, then there might still be contrary imaginations. The imagination could contrive a problem all by itself. So, Constantin observed, it is what the imagination brings to a problem which shapes the problem. Alex was beginning to see parallels between Constantin's adventures and his own. The brown cardboard box meant something different to each one of them.

The sound from the television intensified, and Alex knew it was commercial time. Joel's appearance in the kitchen confirmed it. Joel took the cardboard carton of cold milk from the refrigerator and placed it on the end of the table. He reached for a glass from the cupboard. He picked up the plastic chocolate syrup container, also, but Mom shook her head, and he put it back. Slowly he poured the cold milk. But if he didn't move faster, the commercial would end before he got back to the television.

Then Alex saw Joel glancing sideways at Mom, and he knew Joel wasn't in any hurry to get back to the television.

"Mom," Joel said.

"Yes?" She had lost the game of solitaire and was scraping the cards into a single pile.

Now that he had her attention, Joel seemed reluctant to speak. He sipped at the cold milk, put it down, glanced again at the chocolate syrup, but didn't give serious consideration to another effort in that direction.

"Mom, you know one of my favorite places in the whole wide world?"

"The sofa in front of the television?" Alex said, smiling, and then regretted he had said it. He wasn't trying to be unkind.

Joel ignored him. "It's the park, Mom. We can walk to the park from here, and it's bright green. A peanut butter sandwich tastes better if you eat it on the park bench beneath that big green pine tree than it tastes any other place in the whole wide world." He sipped at the cold milk again. Alex began to see the direction Joel's mind was moving.

"Mom, Dad loved it under that big pine tree. At least you said he did. You said we used to have boiled shrimp and crab suppers there. Isn't that right Mom? When you sit on that picnic bench, you can practically see a mile. All the way over to the carousel. It's a wonderful place to see things from, isn't it, Mom?"

Slowly Mom shuffled the cards she held in her hand.

"Yes, Joel, it is."

"Mom, that's where Dad wants to be buried. I know it."

She carefully straightened the edges of the pack of cards and placed them on the table before her.

"I never thought about it before, Joel. It is a lovely place. Your dad did like it a lot. You might be right, Joel. We ought to talk about it."

A Different
Point of View

Finally Alex remembered he still hadn't called
Tisha. They were the same age. They had
known each other forever. She lived just down the
block. He knew she was his friend. But she was
more than that. She was someone he would ride a
bicycle all the way to Shreveport for.

She had dark red hair, like his father's, which showed tints of gold when the sun was just right. She had a delicate nose and a pointed chin, but a full jaw and full red lips. She had long, slender fingers, and she used them to tinkle the piano keys and strum the guitar and occasionally the mandolin. Alex liked best the cadence of the Spanish songs. Alex had clutched those slender fingers tenderly when the two of them took long walks, but he had never dared kiss those full red lips.

They sat on the shore of the green pond in the park, watching the ducks frolic. Tisha had brought slices of bread, and she shared a slice with Alex. They broke the bread in small pieces and tossed the pieces across the water toward the ducks.

"Big Al's right, Alex," said Tisha.

"Sure he is."

"Alex, maybe your mother's looking for answers to questions which don't exist." She broke off a piece of bread, moved her arm back to throw it into the pond, then had second thoughts, and the bread touched her lips. She chewed daintily. "Let's play a game. Suppose we are your father. He isn't well. Everything you've said tells me he loved your mother and he loved his children. And he's dying. Alex, you and I are dying. What do we feel? He wants to be with your mother, Alex. He wants to be with you and the twins. But he wants to be in your mind, not in your living room.''

That was the same kind of thought Big Al had, but different. It made sense.

''Alex, suppose you are your father.'' She gazed out over the pond. The ducks waited patiently to be fed, but Tisha's mind now moved on a different plane. ''Suppose you are ashes in a box on a table in the front room. How would you feel each time someone walked through the room?''

Alex hadn't thought about what was happening from his father's point of view. He had thought about things from the point of view of all the living. But who's to say if ashes in a cardboard box don't also have a point of view? The father he had known wouldn't have wanted to be on display on a table in the front room, people gawking and saying, ''Oh, Lord!'' The father he knew would have wanted to be remembered with love.

"I love you, Tisha," said Alex.

"What?"

"You heard me. You just want to hear it again."

"Oh, Alex, you're always out in left field some-where. Probably we have loved each other since first grade. What has that got to do with what we are talking about now?"

"I guess I never dared say it before."

Tisha threw the last piece of bread to the one hungry duck remaining. She reached over and touched Alex's cheek with a slender finger. Then she stood up, dusted off her skirt, smiled at him, and moved back toward the path, a thin, curled finger beckoning him to follow.

"Your mom needs help, Alex. You are the only one who can give her that help. What is it your fa-ther wanted? You are him, and he is you. You're the one who has to find out. I'll help if you want me to," she said.

Advance Notice
for a Funeral

First the doorbell rang, then there was an insistent knock on the door, then a banging. Alex barely knew the tall, skinny lady who was doing the knocking, but he surely knew the heavyset Father Tom Fulsome, who stood right behind her.

"Boy," she said, "where's your mama?"

By that time Alex's mother was standing behind him.

"My daughter says there's a dead man in this house!"

Father Tom put his hands on her shoulders and moved her aside, gently, but firmly.

"Mary Dorothy, you have a minute?"

Father Tom wasn't a stranger to this house. Fact is, he was probably Big Al's best friend. Mom and Alex had shared gallons of lukewarm coffee with Big Al and Father Tom.

Mom smiled and nodded and held the door open.

It was an uncomfortable time for the tall, skinny lady and the short, plump priest, but soon they sat on the living room couch, stirring coffee, and Alex wondered what would happen next.

It started out quietly. The lady spoke. "My daughter was here earlier. She said there is a dead man in this house. Is that true?"

Alex had seen her in church. Always in the first pew. She was concerned about folding her hands tight in prayer, and she was concerned about singing the hymns in as loud a voice as possible. She wasn't very good at singing, but Alex was beginning to think maybe it was trying that deserved best marks. At least that was part of what Constantin seemed to be saying.

Father Tom tried his very best to take charge. "Mary Dorothy, what's going on?"

Alex's mom told him. The lady's eyes widened. She twisted on a handkerchief until it was almost a piece of string. Father Tom had problems with his tight white collar.

"Mary Dorothy, I'm so sorry about what is happening to you and your family. If there's any way I can help, you tell me." He stuck a finger behind his collar and fiddled with it some more.

But that wasn't what the tall, skinny lady wanted to hear. "My daughter won't even eat my fine cooking, she is so frightened. Now, what are you going to do about that?"

Mom was more interested in getting a message across to Father Tom than in helping the lady fatten up her skinny daughter. "We'll decide tomorrow. Is that soon enough?"

"I knew I could count on you, Mary Dorothy."

Father Tom took the tall, skinny lady by the elbow and ushered her across the porch and down
the steps. He spun his head to look back at Alex's
mother.

"Mary Dorothy, what is it exactly that you plan to
do? If the Church is to be involved in a burial, we
need some kind of advance notice."

Mom nodded.

"I'll call you," she said.

That seemed to satisfy Father Tom, although it
certainly didn't satisfy the tall, skinny lady. Father
Tom had hold of her arm as they marched down the
sidewalk, but he wasn't in control of her. She knew
where she was headed, and that's where she went.

Somebody Better
Do Something

"Walter's mother said I could play over his house, but he couldn't play over my house," said Joel.

It was a pain of a day and getting worse, thought Alex. Already Tisha had volunteered to unravel a problem she couldn't possibly help solve. Father

Tom had tried to ward off another problem and failed miserably.

Now, Mom tried to solve Joel's problem by calling Walter's mother. Alex sat and listened. He knew his mother would rather have privacy, but he wanted to hear the conversation, and it would be more honest to sit where she could see him than to leave the room and listen just outside the door.

"That's right," Mom said into the phone softly.

"That's right," she said again.

"That's right," she said a third time, "and be advised that it is none of your business, and you can tell your snotty-nosed little son that Joel has other friends whose parents have something more than head colds between their ears." Her voice was still soft as she put down the phone, but her eyes were slits of anger.

She pivoted and saw Alex.

"That really felt good," she said.

Nothing more happened until the middle of the afternoon, when Lily and her friend Gretchen came in the back door. Lily carried pen and writing pad. Gretchen clutched a small camera.

Gretchen gave Alex a shy smile. "I'm not supposed to be here," she said.

"Why?" asked Alex, not because he didn't know.

"You know," said Gretchen, pointing toward the front room.

"Would you like to see the box?"

"That's why we're here, Alex," said Lily. "Where's Mom?"

Lily looked at the clock on the kitchen wall. "Well, it's long past her nap time. Mom!" she yelled, walking toward Mom's bedroom.

"What's going on?" Alex asked Gretchen.

"Show-and-tell," said Gretchen.

"What?"

"I think we could both get an A if we could get an interview and some pictures," she said.

The noise from the bedroom got progressively louder. Then Lily came tromping into the kitchen, yelling back over her thin shoulder, "All right, Mom, but silence just isn't God's way. That's why they have bells and organs and singing and praying out loud in church."

Lily glared at Alex as she passed.

"Come on, Gretchen," she ordered.

Quiet again. Mom's afternoon nap stretched out. She needed it, thought Alex. He decided he would play policeman should anyone else come marching in.

There was a tap at the back door. It was Tisha.

"I thought you might need company," she said.

Alex told her about Joel and Walter and about Lily and Gretchen. She smiled because Alex was making light of both incidents. He could see that to her they weren't funny.

"Would you like some root beer?" he asked.

She nodded. It was also obvious she wasn't particularly thirsty. She was being polite.

"I talked to my father," she said.

Alex knew her father, but not really well. Her father liked sports because he attended all the school ball games, and he taught something at the junior college.

"He treats everything as if it were a problem in a school textbook," Tisha continued. "He said when a family has a problem and doesn't do anything about it, that's the worst kind of problem to have. Then he started writing down numbers and talking about how the same laws apply to physics as apply to psychology, and I decided I could wait until I got to college to learn what he was talking about."

She hadn't touched the root beer, but she was staring at it.

"Alex, what he was *trying* to say wasn't all that hard to figure out. Somebody's got to do something."

"You want some more root beer?" Alex asked.

Her eyes lifted. She had not taken a single sip from her root beer. She tightened her lips.

"That's not funny, Alex. You don't want me to help, I won't help." She stood up, hesitated, then sat down again.

"I'm not leaving," she said. "We don't have to talk about this anymore. What do you want to talk about?"

Alex thought for a moment. There was something he wanted to talk about.

"Let's take a walk," he said.

≈ C H A P T E R   1 8 ≈

One Word
Solves the Problem

Alex didn't even know if there was a reason why he suggested they walk toward the Danneel Street Cemetery. He had always thought of this cemetery as his link with the past. Three generations of relatives on his father's side were buried here. Someday Granny Victoria would take her place beside Grandpa. And when Mom's time came, she would be buried here, too. He seldom took it past that point. Somewhere inside, he knew he might also be buried here or someplace close. There was comfort in the idea, although he wasn't sure why.

It was an aboveground cement box called a copen (he had looked up the word), cement walls painted with whitewash. It was a cement resting place about the size of a cement double bed. He touched the coldness of the cement. The cement walls were filled with dirt, and the dirt was filled with Grandpa, and memories of Grandpa, and family stories—some Alex had heard, some only hinted at. At the head of the cement tomb was a flat marblelike stone with names and dates. People. Born one date. Dead the next. Cold cement. No mistaking the idea.

Tisha had never been there before, and she stood back and stared. Alex moved closer, viewing the well-kept grave, saying a quiet prayer for his grandfather. At the very last second he remembered to include his father.

Across the walk was a small grassy area with a bench on three sides. Alex motioned Tisha toward the benches.

"Want to talk here, or should we go someplace else?" he asked.

She answered by sitting on one of the benches. He sat beside her and handed her *Contrary Imaginations*.

"The guy in this book is kind of different. He goes around challenging all of the rules. And I guess before it's all over, he'll get into trouble because of that. But the part I like best is that he goes exploring places where you don't expect to find rules, like in dreams. He goes there looking for rules to be challenged.

"The part I'm reading right now is about . . . well, it's like, uh . . . if you think you're going to feel bad, then you will feel bad. And if . . ." Alex looked around, searching for something. His eyes lit on a wildflower growing beside the bench, and he broke the stem off near the ground and held it out to Tisha.

"What kind of flower is this?"

"A buttercup."

"Well, if you think that a buttercup is the most beautiful flower in the whole wide world, then it is."

"As a matter of fact," said Tisha, "this *is* the most beautiful flower in the world. I've always thought so. It's simple, and it has a delicate smell, and you can find it whenever you want it."

"Right. Now, why do you think this particular flower grew right here? Did we know we'd be sitting here and do something to make sure it would be here when we got here?"

Tisha smiled. "I like playing these kinds of games, Alex, as long as you don't get too serious about it."

"I'm just trying to give you an idea what the book is about. Constantin seems to keep saying over and over that most times we can be what we want to be and that things can be what we want them to be. Not always, but never if we don't try."

Tisha had closed her eyes. It was unlikely that she was sleeping, but she didn't seem to be listening. It was as if her undivided attention were on the fragrance of the buttercup.

That's when Alex saw Constantin.

He was sitting on the bench across the small green lawn. He looked just like the picture Alex had formed in his mind. Broad shoulders. Clean-shaven.

There was a wry smile on his face, as though he had been listening to Alex muddlingly paraphrase the thoughts he expressed in the book. What Alex hadn't expected was his clothing. Alex had pictured him in the garb of a Roman warrior. But he was wearing a gray business suit and a maroon tie.

"You picked a good time to show up." But the words stayed in Alex's mind. He dared not say them aloud.

The smile remained on Constantin's face. His lips didn't move. But suddenly there were words in Alex's head.

"You put a lot of stock in that old Chinese person," said Alex, and Constantin appeared to nod.

"But words don't seem to be what's needed here," said Alex.

He could feel the force of the reply. Distant thunder roared. The words of the old Chinese person rumbled in Alex's ears.

"Wrong!" said the old Chinese person. "One word is what is needed to eliminate your distress."

Alex didn't understand. He looked to Constantin for help, but Constantin was looking away from him, toward the cement copen. There were no more words in Alex's head, and yet he felt something was being said.

"It's you who has to act, Alex," said Tisha, suddenly awake from her reverie. "What are you going to do?"

Alex looked quickly toward Tisha, then back toward Constantin, but Constantin was no longer seated. Now he was walking toward the cemetery entrance. There was a spirit to his walk that said he had other important things to attend to.

Words cluttered Alex's mind, but they weren't Constantin's words. They were Tisha's words.

He stood up, then offered her his hand.

"Time to go, Tisha," he said. "Maybe now I know what to do."

Trying to Control
the Dream

Mary Dorothy's scream shattered the early-morning quiet. Alex bolted out of bed and into the living room.

His mother stood before the homework table in the front room where Alex had placed the cardboard box. But the table was empty.

"Look!" she screamed. "Look!" But there was nothing to look at.

In a moment the twins rushed in, followed by Granny Victoria.

"Mary Dorothy, I need my sleep," Granny said. "What's causing all this noise?"

Mom pointed to the table. It was as if she had no words left.

"The box is gone," Alex said.

Who would have dared move it?

"I know it's gone," said Granny Victoria. "I lay in my bed past midnight, trying to get some sleep. But the thought of my son in that box and that box in this house drove sleep away. I put the box in the trunk of the car, and I've been sleeping soundly ever since."

Mom was composed, but only for a moment.

"Victoria, I'd like you to go and pack your suitcase. If you don't mind, I'm bringing you home. It was a mistake for me to think I could deal with what I'm having to deal with and be a good hostess at the same time."

Alex heard the words. They were rather softly

spoken, but from the way Granny whipped around and headed for her room, he knew they weren't softly received.

"Children," Mom said, "we'll make a day of it. Bring your bathing suits if you like. I'm going to call Big Al and ask if he will drive. I don't think I'm up to more of Granny Victoria's driver education."

After breakfast they loaded the car. Granny's suitcase went in the trunk next to the cardboard box. Lily carried a package under her arm.

"Lily, we're hard-pressed for room," said Mom.

"Mom, I really want to take my radio-tape player." She squeezed the package in the trunk.

"Lily," said Joel, "bring the player in the car. We could hear some music."

"I need to get batteries," said Lily, carefully closing the lid to the trunk.

Big Al, Mom, and Joel took the front seat. Alex and Lily took a window in the backseat, with Granny in the middle.

Big Al slowly backed the car out of the driveway.

"Watch it! Car coming down the road," said Granny.

But after that for a while things were quiet. Alex opened his book again. Constantin sat on the shore of a sea, the waters of which were as white and thick as milk. He said he planned to watch and to meditate. He advised the reader to do the same. Surely other strange things were about to happen.

"Beep!" went Joel's computer game.

"Mom!" said Lily.

Mom ignored them both.

"Who'd like some boiled shrimp once we get to your grandmother's?" asked Big Al.

"I don't feel much like boiling shrimp," said Granny Victoria. Alex knew she resented being sent home and was telling Mom so.

"Well," said Big Al, "I'm the best cook there is when it comes to boiling water. I'll do the work, and you do the eating."

Everybody approved of that. Alex went back to his book. Constantin was discussing meditation with the old Chinese person. But something was nudging for Alex's attention in the real world. He closed the covers of the book and listened. Mom was talking to Big Al about a dream she had last night.

"I had to go someplace," she said. "I'd been there before. The streets were all familiar to me. But every street I took was the wrong one."

"You're under a lot of pressure right now, Mary Dorothy. That's all your dream was trying to tell you," said Big Al.

And then a string of trucks began to pass. Granny Victoria tensed but didn't say anything. The words coming from the front seat came to Alex's ears in spurts, always incomplete.

". . . problem solvers . . ."

". . . analyzing the dream . . ."

". . . learning to control the dream . . ."

". . . just another way to test the rules . . ."

What was Alex hearing? It was Big Al talking, but it was Constantin talking, also. How could that be? Maybe Big Al had read the book. Maybe both Big Al and Constantin read the same books.

From where he was sitting, Alex could see Big Al only in profile. Even when Big Al turned his head slightly to look at Mom, Alex couldn't read his expression.

Alex's mind went back to the cemetery. He mentally examined Constantin's face. Then he mentally examined Big Al's face. Not a single feature matched. Only their words matched.

Alex returned to the book. Moments later he had completed the final page. It was a helpful book.

Alex's gaze was on Big Al. For the first time he began looking at Big Al as a permanent member of the family. Constantin had a bunch of the answers. They were revealing.

Big Al might have even more.

Mostly True Confessions

They walked up the sandy steps and in the front door of Granny Victoria's, and Big Al took charge. An hour later the center of the oilcloth covered kitchen table was piled high with pink and steaming boiled shrimp. A frosty pitcher of homemade root beer laced with ice cubes sat on each end of the table.

Noises of chairs being pulled closer to the table filled the air.

"Where's Lily?" Mom asked, but as she asked, Lily walked into the room.

"We can talk while we eat," said Granny Victoria. There were more eating noises than talking noises.

Alex loved boiled shrimp. He was skilled at peeling off the shell. Down went the shrimp into the hot sauce. Up went the shrimp to his mouth. The taste was delicious. Even the chewing was a joy.

Lily was carefully peeling shrimp and placing them in a bowl. When the bowl was full, she would begin to eat, taking one shrimp at a time, daintily dipping it in catsup lightly flavored with hot sauce, then taking a tiny bite. She always ate shrimp this way. Alex envied her self-control as the peeled shrimp began to fill the bowl.

Mary Dorothy ate a few of the shrimp, dabbed at the corners of her mouth with a napkin, picked up another shrimp, then put it down.

"Victoria, I've decided to bury the ashes in the family plot. I know that's all right with you, but it somehow seemed right to wait and tell you here."

Alex shuddered. He had known this time would come. He had never figured a way to avoid it or to cope with it. And so now he must tell the truth.

"Mom . . ."

She looked in his direction. "One minute, Alex." Her attention went back to Granny Victoria. "It *is* all right with you, isn't it?"

"Surely, dear. It's the right place for him," said Granny Victoria.

"Good."

"Mom . . ."

A tenseness seemed to leave Mary Dorothy as she faced Alex.

"What is it, Alex? More hot sauce?"

He backed his chair from the table, started to stand, then thought the better of it.

"Mom, Dad's already buried in the family plot. I couldn't stand it anymore with him in the front room. I did it in the middle of last night. I said a prayer over him for all of us."

In the hush that followed, he told them about taking from the cardboard box a white plastic bag filled with ashes and substituting a white plastic bag filled with dirt.

Alex had expected anger, but that was not what he got.

Mom stood up slowly, tears streaming down her cheeks. Her voice was soft.

"Oh, Alex, you had no right to do that."

Big Al reached for her hand. She sat back down, used the napkin to dry her tears, but the tears wouldn't stop flowing.

"At least he is where you want him to be," said Big Al.

"Mom?"

It was Joel. Alex looked toward him. Joel was sobbing tears of his own.

"It's all right, son," she said. "We'll talk to Father Tom and have a regular service at the cemetery."

"But Daddy's not buried in the cemetery, Mom," said Joel. "Last night I buried him in the park near the big pine tree."

He quickly stood up, rushed around the table, and threw his arms around Mom. "Mom, I'm so sorry," he sobbed.

Mom held him tight for a long time, then slowly moved him arm's length away.

"Oh, dear boy. It's all right, Joel. This is truly my fault. If I hadn't been so indecisive about what to do with your father, none of this would have happened." She looked toward Big Al as if seeking strength. Then her eyes returned to Joel.

"I think, son, that your father would be proud that you did what you thought he wanted you to do. But for all of us, it would be better that he be in a less public place than the park. We'll have the ashes moved from the park to the cemetery."

It was quiet.

"Anybody still hungry?" asked Granny Victoria. "We haven't even made a dent in that pile of shrimp." She found a big one, and the tiny, crisp sound of the shell cracking was the only sound to be heard.

Then Lily spoke. "Mom, I think that there is one more thing you should know."

"Lord, Lily, I've learned so much in the last few minutes."

"Daddy isn't buried in the park, either, Mom. While you-all were boiling the shrimp, I buried Daddy's ashes out on the beach, which is where God kind of told me Daddy truly wanted to be."

What Happened
April 3?

Laughter bubbled deep inside Alex. It got bigger and bubblier, but even with his lips held tightly shut, a giggle trickled out.

"Don't you dare laugh at me, Alex. I only did what I thought Dad, and I'm pretty sure God, wanted me to do."

Then Mom smiled, and Big Al just plain laughed, and Joel snickered, and even Granny Victoria's eyes twinkled, and Lily didn't stay mad. But she didn't crack a smile, either.

"Well, for sure we know your father was loved," said Big Al. "But it also shows what can happen when people go around thinking they know what's best for everybody else."

Granny Victoria poured her glass full of root beer. An ice cube slid from pitcher to glass, splashing root beer on the table, and she wiped at it with her napkin.

"Anything like this ever happen again, you children talk to your mama first," she said sternly, and at first there was a stillness, but then genuine laughter bounced again around the table.

"Okay, now," said Big Al. "It's part funny and part not. Your father's buried someplace, and maybe we ought to find out where." He gave a little snicker, looked at Mary Dorothy, and his face quickly became serious.

"If Lily just buried him this morning, then he can't be buried on the beach," said Joel. "I buried him last night."

But Alex knew there were pieces missing. "The important thing isn't *when* we buried him," said Alex. "It's whoever was first to take the real ashes and substitute the dirt."

"That's right, Alex," said Big Al, waiting for Alex to continue. Alex was deep in thought, so Big Al's attention shifted to Joel.

"When did you do it, Joel?"

"April third," said Joel.

"Me, too," said Lily.

Everyone's eyes were on Alex.

"Me, too," he said.

"Why April third?" asked Big Al.

"It was his birthday," said Mary Dorothy. "I thought long and hard myself about making the right decision on that day."

"So now it boils down to the time of day," said Big Al, his eyes on each child in turn.

All three remembered that it was after everyone else had gone to sleep, but nobody had seen a clock. All three had made their plans the day before, the dirt already packaged in the white plastic bag. All three had silently slipped into the front room, made the substitution, and left. Alex had hidden his bag behind *Contrary Imaginations* on the bookshelf in his room. Joel had hidden his bag in the video game drawer before burying it in the park. Lily had hidden her bag in a shoe box under her bed, then in the package with the radio-tape player in the trunk of the car.

"Lordy," said Big Al, "it was like a shopping mall in that room, people coming in and out at all hours but not making a sound."

"Big Al, what am I going to do?" asked Mary Dorothy.

Big Al smiled gently at her. "It's not that difficult a problem, Mary Dorothy." He surveyed the group. When his eyes focused on Alex and Alex smiled back, Big Al nodded. "Tell your Mom what to do, Alex."

That was another reason why Alex liked Big Al.

"Mom, I can think of two things to do. One is easy. The other is hard. We can dig up what Lily and Joel buried and rebury it in the family plot. Then for sure we would know where most of Dad was.

"Or we can leave things just like they are. When

we are at the beach, if we want to, we can think Dad is here with us. Same for the park. Same for the cemetery."

Would the whole family think the same as he did?

"But, Mom, the minute I finished putting what I thought was Dad in the ground, something happened to me. I didn't think of him anymore as being in the ground. I didn't think of him anymore as being ashes. He's in my head. He is a part of me. And he'll be with me forever, no matter where I am or where he is," said Alex.

"Me, too," said Joel.

"Me, too," said Lily.

"And I guess me, too," said Mom. She looked first at Joel, then Lily, then Alex. Then Big Al. She toyed with a boiled shrimp. "All right. Since this sits well with all of us, then we'll leave your dad right where he is. Wherever that is. He wants us to remember him but to move on." She tilted her head and smiled a pretty smile at Big Al.

"But, Mom," said Lily, "I just thought of something."

This time Alex was a mile ahead of her. Lily was thinking what God would say about three funerals and Father Tom Fulsome not being at a single one of them.

Alex reached over, unscrewed the cap off the red-hot sauce, and dumped it all in the bowl of Lily's delicious, freshly peeled shrimp. He sensed her scream of anguish before it came. Her full attention was now on the loss of all those tasty shrimp. And that's exactly what Alex wanted.

Probably, Alex thought, and smiled happily at the thought, God wanted it that way, also.

≈ C H A P T E R 2 2 ≈

Two Fathers
Are Better Than One

They journeyed home in the afternoon. That night sleep wouldn't come for Alex. There was still unfinished business.

Alex knew what he wanted to say so clearly the ballpoint pen carved the words onto the page. He tiptoed to his mother's room. The lamp on her bedside table glowed dimly. He could hear soft breathing. He carefully placed the note on the table and backed out of the light.

"Mom," the note said, "Dad is where you want him to be. Only a dimwit"—on second reading he had scratched out "dimwit" and substituted "child"—"wouldn't be able to tell the difference between the weight of ashes and the weight of dirt."

Back in his room his bed felt cool and soft. Sleep time.

One final thought whispered for his attention.

Maybe sometimes, with Dad in memory and Big Al here, maybe sometimes two fathers *are* better than one.